the lesson

a student-teacher romantic suspense

TL MAYHEW

Prologue

Winston Asher Harrington III

MY FINGERS STRUM NERVOUSLY atop the worn pine table. Its surface scarred from what I imagine is years of individuals pleading innocence and spewing obscenities at a fatigued agent on the opposite side, unaffected by the outburst.

Innocent until proven guilty is what they always say.

Except in my case, I am guilty.

No matter how much I try to forget, the memory of what I've done consumes me, and the only way to overcome this burden is to turn myself in. I realize the consequences could mean prison time. But it's better than spending an eternity with this weight on my shoulders.

So here I sit, waiting.

I've memorized every scuff, crack, and imperfection on the four dingy white walls of this temporary cage while avoiding the elephant in the room, a two-way mirror. It tempts me like a scantily clad teenage girl in a high school classroom.

I know they're watching. They're always watching. But if I give in, taking even the slightest glance, they'll see right through my façade. Instead, I focus on a red splotch, no bigger than a pencil eraser, and let my mind wander. Is it blood? DNA left by a stranger who sat in this very chair and stared at the same four white walls? Or is it something less impressive, like ink from a marker? I shrug, arching my back slightly.

Hours have passed since they brought me in, and my spine aches from years of proper etiquette training ingrained in my mind from the tender age of six. If I slouch even the slightest, my muscles tense, preparing for the crack of my father's belt while his bold voice rings in my ears. *"Sit up straight."*

He's dead now, and I refuse to waste my thoughts on him, but his discipline will forever live on in the deepest part of my brain.

A glance at the clock tells me I've been waiting far too long. I can't sit any longer. I need to get up and stretch my legs. So, I do. Since they haven't read me my Miranda Rights, I'm able to move freely about the room. Every so often bending and touching my toes to stretch out stiff muscles.

Standing straight, I twist my body from side to side, and think about why I'm here. Legally, I could leave. If there was anything substantial on me, I'd be in cuffs right now. Instead, they're making me sweat it out, hoping to get a confession. Little do they know I was ready to confess the instant they sat me down in this room, but their tactics aren't working. It's just the opposite. *The longer I wait, the less interest I have in telling them anything.* I think to myself.

The thought flits from my mind as quickly as it came when the door opens and in walks two men—dressed in jeans and button-down dress shirts, each with a badge suspended from a chain and lying flat against their chests.

It's no secret who's a good cop from the bad. The older gentleman is ten or so years older than me. His face creased with years of fighting bad guys while the younger guy appears just out of high school. I believe he and I had been in Mr. Gantry's class together.

"Lance? Lance Freeman, is that you?" I ask, crossing my arms and challenging his authority.

He counters by stiffening his stance. "Detective Freeman to you, Mr. Harrington. Please, take a seat. My partner, Detective Winslow, and I have some questions to ask."

Detective? How is that possible? Lance and I didn't graduate but four years ago, and while I knew very little of him then, I would've surely heard if he'd finished college. Hell, there would've been a parade. It's the one thing you can be sure of living in the town of Silvercrest. Any achievement is an excuse for a black-tie celebration, just like the masquerade ball hosted by the mayor over the weekend.

If he's made detective already, it means there was money involved.

I eye him cautiously, curious about his status and about what they might have on me, but his expression is that of a poker player and gives nothing away. Finding out my fate will mean more time in the cold metal folding chair. Reluctantly, I take a seat. "Well, get on with it then. I have homework to grade and tests to plan for tomorrow's classes."

Lance settles in the seat across from me while Detective Winslow perches a cheek on the edge of the table in front. Intimidation is his intent, but it has little effect. In my line of work, thick skin is a requirement. Teenagers are not kind people, especially those with money.

"Mr. Harrington, do you know why you're here?" Detective Winslow asks.

I have my suspicions, but there's no way I'm drawing attention to the fact. "Not specifically, no."

He nods. "Detective Freeman, show him the pictures."

The young detective sets a folder—I hadn't realized he was holding—on the table. When he opens it, a school picture of Catarina Mills is the first photo I see. Although, it's in black and white, her fair hair and bright smile doesn't get lost in the colorless image. On the honor roll and class president, she's an outgoing and well-liked senior. She's also one of my students.

He slides the image across the table. "Do you recognize her?"

"Yes. That's Catarina Mills. Her friends call her Rina," I affirm with a nod.

"Can you tell us how you know Miss Mills?" the aged detective questions.

I shift in my seat, unsure of where this line of questioning is going, because it's not what I thought. "She's taking my English literature class. Why?"

Silence thickens the air and a look passes between the two men, before Detective Winslow says, "Show him."

My breath catches at the next image slid across the table. It's of a young woman lying in a field. Her school-issued blouse is disheveled and gapes open, exposing her bra, while her skirt lies across her stomach, and her panties are missing. Purple hues paint her skin at the wrists and ankles, inferring she'd been restrained at some point. A quick glance at her face suggests the lifeless body is Catarina's.

Bile rises in my throat and I turn away. This situation is a lot more serious than I thought.

Chapter 1

Francis Harlyn Aldridge

ONE WEEK AGO...

"So...did you try it?"

Taking a quick look around, I make sure no one is listening before leaning in toward Quinn's desk. "Dude, he didn't even get the head in before I was begging for him to stop. There is no fucking way people enjoy that."

She laughs, but not a quiet don't-draw-attention-to-us laugh; it's a howl capable of calling a pack of wolves, and everyone in class turns. With their collective eyes on us, heat tints my cheeks, and I want to crawl under the desk, but I don't. If I show any trace of weakness, my popularity will fizzle straight into the hands of Catarina Mills, and that's not something I'm prepared to give up, especially not to her. No, I hold my ground and laugh right along with Quinn, even if my own laugh is as fake as the brand-new tits my mom got last year.

Once we've quieted and the class has lost interest, she continues, "Just keep trying, you may not think so now, but eventually, you'll be begging for it."

"I highly doubt it. This weekend was a mistake. I can't keep going back, otherwise, he's going to get the wrong idea."

Fanning out her fingers, she checks the perfectly polished nails before her tired eyes meet mine. "You should keep hold of that leash for as long as you can; there's nothing wrong with using someone to get laid now and again, at least until someone better comes along."

"Ladies, I hope I'm not interrupting," Mr. Harrington cuts in, a hint of annoyance teasing his tone. Even though he's addressing us both, his hard stare is pinned on me, as if I said something to offend him.

At this point I could care less if I did because those hazel eyes, combined with the deep timber in his voice, send chills over my skin, making it impossible to think I didn't notice him approach—something which is so unlike me along with every other girl in this class. We can't call it a day in English without scoping out the door every afternoon, waiting for the hottest teacher in school to step through.

Today, he's in a fitted chinos and a white dress shirt. Some may think it's dull, but he once told us he dresses in the school uniform to fit in. Puts him at our level, but I say far from it. With the five o'clock shadow on his strong jawline and thick wavy hair that I'd love to run my hands through, there is no hiding that kind of sexy. And don't even get me started on his glasses.

The thought of him hearing our conversation...well, let's just say, if my cheeks were heated before, they're on fire now. I bite my lower lip and lower my eyes. "No, sir."

Quinn, not one to shy away from confrontation, is unapologetic for the disturbance; instead, she shows a little more leg and flutters her lashes. "Winston, you look especially nice today. Is that a new tie?"

"Thank you, Miss Raynor, no, it's not. And once again, call me Mr. Harrington," he corrects, tapping his fingers on her desk before addressing the rest of the students. "Class, I'd like you all to take your seats and open your books to Act IV. For scenes I, II, and III, once you've read through, close your books, and we'll talk through what you think Shakespeare is leading up to at this point in the play."

There's a shuffle of book bags and the grind of chairs across the wooden floor as everyone settles in. I do the same, reaching down for my own, fumbling through until I find my copy of Hamlet. When I rise back up, I'm shocked to find him leaning over me. He's so close the heat of his forearm warms my back, and I see his knuckles whiten as his fingers press against my desk.

I clear the knot in my throat and chance a glance at him, but instantly wish I hadn't. The look of disappointment on his beautiful features make my stomach sink.

"Stop by my desk after class today, Harlyn," he orders me and, without further explanation, heads to the front of the room.

There's no asking if I'm available or if I could set aside some time later in the week, it's more an order, one that should annoy me but has the opposite effect. The thought of being alone with Mr. Harrington sends a wave of need straight down to my core.

"Hmmm, is he extra fucking hot today, or is it just me?" Quinn sighs, fanning herself and pulling me from my teacher's dream.

The question is rhetorical, but I answer anyway. "It's not just you," I mutter.

"What'd he want anyway? A quickie in the teachers' lounge?"

My eyes snap to hers.

"Fuck...No. Really?" she asks excitedly.

This time, it's my turn to laugh. I know she's not that gullible, but it's fun to tease. "Of course not. He did tell me to stop by after class, though." I offer her a wink before casually turning in my seat and opening my book.

"Bitch, you have got to get you some of that. He's ten times hotter than that loser Lance, and you can bet Mr. Harrington has popped a few virgin ass cherries in his time."

"Quinn!" I gasp, embarrassed. "Shut up! I don't need the whole fucking class to know about it."

She leans in and whispers, "You'd better give me all the details."

It's probably nothing, or I suppose it could be about my grades. With Lance suspiciously showing up wherever I go, I haven't been doing much studying. Usually, it wouldn't be a big deal, since bribing the teachers in this place for anything higher than a C is considered normal. But Mr. Harrington is a hard ass and isn't easily swayed. My parents have already tried.

"I'm sure it's not like that," I correct, lifting my eyes to the front where I catch him staring. Most would look away, but he doesn't. His eyes stay on mine as he stretches back in his chair and places his hands behind his head. Maybe it is like that.

I shift in my seat, causing the hem of my skirt to ride higher on my thighs. If it were any other man, they'd chance a glance, but I know he won't. Something is intriguing and sexy about having such control. I'd never really noticed that about him before.

Just as I consider dropping my hand beneath the desk and satisfying this sudden onset of need—giving him a real show—a timer goes off. It breaks our connection, and he clears his throat pulling his attention back to the rest of the classroom. "So, who can tell me how far you've gotten, and what do you think the author was thinking at this point in the story?"

A slurry of perfectly manicured nails shoot skyward as soon as the words leave his lips. It's their chance to impress him, even though the majority will not deliver even the slightest inkling of what the story is about. Which is fine because it means he'll spend another twenty minutes explaining his view, and we can watch him pace about the front.

"Rebecca, how about you go first?" he asks.

She giggles and shifts in her seat at the fact he's paying attention to her. "Okay, Mr. Harrington. I made it to scene II. In summary, it seems that Hamlet has killed someone, and the king and queen feel he's crazy."

I'm oblivious to whatever else she says, since all I can think about is what Mr. Harrington wants after class.

Is it about my grades?

Am I in trouble?

How did I not know his lips move like that when he speaks?

"Harlyn, how about you?"

"Umm, what?" Random giggles come from the other girls, and I pin a narrowed stare on them. "Could you please repeat the question, Mr. Harrington?"

He shakes his head. "Pay attention, please. Catarina, can you enlighten Miss Aldridge on what I've asked?"

"I'd be happy to."

I'd be happy to. I scrunch my nose and mock her in my mind.

After repeating the question with a snark that makes me want to punch her in the face, she begins to explain her thoughts on each scene. But she doesn't stop there. Spiraling into a black hole of her thoughts on the entire story, she eats up the rest of our class time, talking nonstop until the bell cuts her off.

I should feel some sense of relief it's over, but my heart is racing, and a million things are spinning through my mind as I watch each student exit the room. This is it—quality time with the man, I lie awake thinking about, every night before I bed.

"Definitely DO everything I would do," Quinn states, eyeing me and then Mr. Harrington.

I smack her on the arm. "Would you get out of here?"

"Gladly," she quips, sauntering toward the front of the room. "See you tomorrow, Winston."

"Quinn, I'm not sure what you get away with in other classes, but here, I'd like to be addressed as Mr. Harrington," he corrects her once again, this time the annoyance profound in his tone.

Quinn is one of my best friends, but sometimes, she can be a total bitch, and now is one of those times. Hearing his name roll off her tongue sends a twinge of jealousy straight to my gut. It's stupid. He's never shown any interest in either of us, but if one day he did, it would be her.

Exercising control over my breathing, I gather my things, intent on moving to the front since no other kids are here, but as I'm bent over, I don't notice his approach and when I upright myself, I bump right into him.

His strong hands grip my arms to keep me from falling back into the chair, and I crane my neck to meet his eyes.

Heat flushes my cheeks. If a hole opened up in the floor right now, I'd be more than happy for it to swallow me up. But it doesn't, and I'm left standing here in the hands of a hot teacher who smells of spicy cologne.

"Hmm, at a loss for words. I find that interesting since you and Miss Raynor talked through my entire class," he comments, taking a moment as his eyes dance between mine, before letting go of my arms and taking a step back. "Please, Miss Aldridge, have a seat."

"I'd rather stand."

Propping himself up on Quinn's desk, he lightly crosses his arms over his chest. "Suit yourself. Do you know why I've kept you after class?"

"No, sir."

Something flashes in his eyes at my response, but it's gone as quickly as it came. "As I'm sure you're aware, your grades are not up to par for the school standards, and that's concerning. Your homework was spot-on at the beginning of the year, and you aced all the tests. Now...you'll be lucky to pass. And if I'm being honest here, it's going to impact your ability to graduate." He shifts against the desk, crossing his feet at the ankles. "Would you like to talk about anything? Maybe problems at home or with a boyfriend?" He spews the last word with a little more grit than necessary.

Is there something going on? I mull over his question. My parents are gone for months at a time; if I don't graduate, I'd lose millions of inheritance money from my grandfather, and I am attracted to my teacher. "Umm, no sir, not really," I tell him, holding his gaze, and wondering how he could be so sure with what's happening in my life.

With a narrowed stare, his expression turns cold. "I'll not tolerate lying in my classroom, Harlyn. I don't see how your grades have dropped so drastically, yet you say nothing is going on. Actually"—he stands and starts walking toward his desk—"maybe you're not ready for my help. You can go."

I scoff at his brush-off. If he doesn't want me here, then I'm not staying, but when I bend to retrieve my bag, images of my parents leaving time after time swirl through my mind. They'd rather be anywhere but here, in Silvercrest with me. If Mr. Harrington is offering to help, and I don't have to go home to an empty house, then why not. Other than Quinn and Lance, I have no one. "There is something."

Mr. Harrington stops mid-step, almost to his desk, but he doesn't turn around. "Go on."

"My parents are out of the country for a while, and without their guidance, I guess, I'm not studying as hard as I should." It's mostly bullshit. I mean, my parents are out of town, but they couldn't care less if I studied or not. I'm going to ace this class, and then once I'm standing on that podium, it'll be the biggest fuck-you they've ever seen.

"Anything else? A boyfriend, maybe?" he repeats his earlier question. There's that word again. Why is he so focused on wanting to know about my *boyfriend*?

Taking a moment, I consider how to answer. It's none of his business, even if my relationship with Lance is a bit rocky right now. I'm not going to tell him anything about us, anyway. With a hand on my hip, I go on the defensive. "And what if I do?"

"Do you spend a lot of time together?" he bites out, turning his now dark eyes and threatening stare on me.

"I guess, but why does that matter?" I ask, offended by his prying.

He takes a step closer, and I drop my bags. If I need to run, there's no fucking way I'm dragging these books with me. "It matters because I'm going to tutor you after school every night until your grade is satisfactory."

"Tutor me? No, that's not going to happen," I argue, taking a step back. "I've got things after school..."

"Like?" He closes in, his aura ever so commanding until the chair hits me in the back of the leg, and I drop into my seat.

I have nothing after school, but I need to make up something and quickly. "Job... yes, I have a job. My parents believe it builds character."

He leans down, one hand on the desk and one on the chair caging me in. I can feel his warm breath on me. "Not anymore, you don't." Grabbing my bag, he sets it on the table. "Tell your parents you're quitting. I'll expect you here after the final bell rings every day for the next two weeks and only at that point will I decide if we need to continue.

"But—"

"Harlyn, it's non-negotiable." With that, he straightens himself and heads toward the door, tossing out, "I'll see you tomorrow afternoon," as he exits the room.

I'm left there, alone and dumbfounded, wondering what the fuck just happened.

Chapter 2

Francis Harlyn Aldridge

WHEN I LEAVE MR. HARRINGTON'S class, the halls are empty. There's still an hour of school left, so everyone is in their last class. Since mine is study hall, I've decided to ditch and just head home. Quinn will be pissed I didn't wait for her, but I don't give a shit. I need to be alone, and think about what just happened with Mr. Harrington.

It's not a minute after I've exited the building when my phone starts chiming.

Him: Hey babe.

Him: U on your way?

It's Lance. I'm supposed to meet him at his place after school, then we'd planned on hanging out by the pool at some friends' house. Well, his friends. I have nothing in common with them, especially when they start drinking. Don't get me wrong, I can hold my liquor with the best of them, but after the day I had, I'm not in the mood for dealing with his handsy friends and a drunk, jealous boyfriend.

He's not the type I'd seen myself with. Bad boys generally aren't my thing. Everyone in this small town knows that in high school, Lance was the epiphany of a bad boy. His days of skipping class and drinking too much got so bad his parents sent him off to a military boot camp.

The reserved town of Silvercrest was much quieter once he left; some were even relieved. Lance isn't an elite, and his presence around those who were, played havoc with The Society parents, including mine. That's when his parents made the decision.

It wasn't until the Mayor was elected recently that Lance was brought home and celebrated a hero. Not because he went to war or anything like that. It was more about him making something of himself. The day he returned is the day he caught my eye. A new man. All man. The uniform didn't hurt, either.

It's always been love for him. When we got together, it wasn't, but a week or two after we started seeing one another, he told me he loved me. At the time, I couldn't bring myself to say it back. For me, it's always been and will probably always be a deep infatuation. I mean, I would do anything for him, and I'd never intentionally hurt him, but love, I'm not sure I see it in our future.

At some point, I need to tell him. Let him decide if he want things to stay the way they are or move on. I'm good either way, but that's not how a relationship should be.

So, I text him back.

Me: School was bullshit.

Me: Headed home.

Me: I'll call later.

While I wait for his reply, Quinn's text pings. Perfect timing, always.

Quinn: Well...

Quinn: Did you fuck him or not?

She's going to judge me whether I answer yes or no, so I type out a quick reply.

Me: Of course not!!!

Me: He's a teacher.

Me: At OUR school.

Quinn: Your point?

She's something else, but I'm not sure what I'd do without her. Friends since childhood, she and I have been inseparable, right up until now. Our time together is falling short. It's something I've meant to ask her, but I've got a lot of things on my mind, and there's no way I can take on the thought of losing my best friend right now. I push the notion from my head and slide into the driver's seat of my Audi TTS, shifting it into drive mode.

The view on the opposite side of my windshield makes up the town of Silvercrest. To an outsider, it's a peaceful place with rolling hills, aged architecture, and perfectly manicured lawns, but beneath the surface are secrets as old as the founding families, secrets known only to the members of The Society.

There are times I wish I didn't know anything about what's happened in the past. With so many lies, cover-ups, and even murders, no one really knows the truth anymore. Just once, I'd like to experience what normal feels like.

The sound of a horn behind me pulls me from my daydream, and I realize the light I'm sitting at has turned green. Luxury cars pass me like I'm standing still as I pull slowly out into the intersection, and begin my drive home.

With the stoplights timed perfectly, it seems everyone is trying to get where they're going, but getting nowhere fast. The traffic inches forward, far enough for me to swerve onto the shoulder and catch the next exit. I take the back road to home, giving me some time to think about what Mr. Harrington had said.

"Tutoring," I repeat the word aloud, cracking through the silence in my car. If anyone in the class finds out, especially Catarina, I'll never hear the end of it. She's always looking for reasons to show everyone how different she is than any of us. But if I don't graduate, I'm screwed, because of a stipulation in my grandfather's will.

A high school diploma and a college degree is a requirement of my trust fund. It's the main reason my parents could care less if I do well in school. Sure, they tried to buy a better grade from Mr. Harrington, but how hard did they press him? My guess is it was one phone call, and they probably didn't even talk with him. Which means they retain control over my multimillion-dollar account.

In Silvercrest, associated with the oldest of old money, is the Aldridge name. Our family has a lineage of wealth, tracing back to books from the 1800s; money earned through years of buying land at pennies on the dollar, then reselling it to railroads, businesses, and even whole towns for double, sometimes almost triple what it originally cost. And as a single child, my father, Harold Mattias Aldridge IV, inherited it all, including the home in which we now live.

Although I am a beneficiary on my father's will, his money is not what's being held hostage by the lack of academic achievements in my hand. No, my trust fund is money from my grandfather on my mother's side. Black River Simmons's money. A small piece of wealth beyond my wildest dreams.

Out of the nine kids he and my grandmother raised, my mother and I were his favorites, and he decided we would be the sole proprietors of everything he built over the past sixty-four years.

As expected, this didn't play out well with the rest of the family, and they disowned us. On occasion, a cousin, uncle, aunt, or even one of my mother's nieces will show up unannounced, and on their best behavior, hoping to get a piece of what doesn't belong to them. It's not hard figuring out their intentions and once we do, my dad has his men send them straight back home.

It's the very reason I need to plow through this English class, and get a high enough grade to graduate because no one is taking what is mine.

Giving this tutoring thing some more thought, ideas roll around in my head about ways we can meet up in private without others knowing. My parents are gone, maybe we could just do it at the house. I shake the thought from my head as quickly as it comes. Even though our home is secluded, we still have neighbors and bored fucking housewives, who don't have anything better to do than gossip.

No, I'll have to think of something else.

When I reach the iron gates that separate our property from the rest of the world, I realize my thoughts have been on everything but the mindless drive I'd hoped to take. It seems if I want any peace of mind, I'll need a session or two with Gunther. Who needs a therapist when you have a masseuse?

I sigh at the thought of setting up some time with him, and my body instantly relaxes, practically melting in my seat. But the feeling is short-lived because the moment I pass through, my phone dings.

Lance: Danny's at seven?

He's persistent, that's for sure, and I'd think by now he'd know better than even to suggest we meet at Danny's. Of all his friends, Danny is the most handsy and aggressively drunk whenever I'm around. There have been times he's even left bruises on my skin, but when I mention it to Lance, he writes it off as harmless flirting.

Nothing about it is harmless or flirtatious. And that means I'm staying away from the situation altogether.

Me: You go. I have cramps.

It's a lie, but I'm not up for any time with him or his friends tonight, and there's no quicker way to end a conversation with a guy than playing that card.

Or so I thought.

His image lights up the screen of my phone. The button on my steering wheel connects us, and his hard tone instantly permeates the interior of my car.

"I'd believe you, if it wasn't only two weeks ago I'd gotten the same excuse."

Dammit.

I heave in a breath and decide to explain. "Lance, I'm sorry, but I just don't like Danny. He's a good guy and all, it's just, how do I say this..."

"Spit it out because I'm interested to hear how Danny is any worse than Quinn. That bitch is the one putting ideas in your head about not wanting to see me, isn't she?" he argues in a seething tone.

"What? No! She didn't say I shouldn't see you." I think back to our conversation in class, and it's just the opposite, but I'm not telling him that. "I've told you about Danny's advances before. Tonight, I'm just not in the mood to fight him off."

"Well I've told you, I talked with him about that. He means no harm. You should feel flattered he shows an interest in you. He's a nice-looking guy and can easily have any girl he wants."

My mouth drops open at his reasoning, it literally renders me speechless. How could I have thought this man is the one I saw myself with? If that's the way he feels, then I need to end this...tonight.

"Harlyn, you still there?"

I take a moment to collect my thoughts, regain my composure and muster up the courage to say what I must. "Lance, we need to talk, but not over the phone. Can you meet me here at the house around six?"

"With bells on," he replies sarcastically, before ending the call.

Glancing down at the blank screen of my phone, I wonder if inviting him to the house was the right decision.

Chapter 3

Francis Harlyn Aldridge

IT'S 5:45 PM, AND THE adrenaline pumping through my veins, is perfectly in sync with each tap of my sandals atop the marble floor in the foyer as I pace between the door and the staircase.

Twenty steps each way is what I've counted.

There's no reason for this type of anxiety. I've tried to end it in the past and was even successful for a few months. But somehow, he always finds a way of pulling me back in. Maybe it's the sex, or perhaps his ability to prey on my one weakness—the fear of being alone.

With parents who never really wanted kids, I've mostly been living the life of an orphan.

Having a child was yet another stipulation of my grandfather's agreement. Mother wouldn't get any of the Simmons' inheritance until she married and produced an offspring. She didn't even get to pick her suitor. An arranged marriage between Silvercrest's Harold Aldridge and Black River's Maria Simmons set forth at the tender ages of twenty-one and eighteen.

Money is a motivator, controlling people's lives and driving their decisions. What the agreement didn't specify is who would raise me.

From the day I was born until my sixteenth birthday, Nanny Grace was like a surrogate mother to me. She still works for us, and I love her to pieces. She's been there for me more than my own mother ever could have been, but as much love as she gives, it'll never fill the hole in my heart as only parents can.

Because of that fear, I'm stuck in a relationship that'll never work. I don't love him and probably never will. He deserves better. Hell, I deserve better. He may not know what's coming, but somehow, I always knew in the back of my mind.

The knock at the door pulls me from my thoughts. He's here. Taking a glance in the entry mirror, I smooth loose strands of hair with my hands and run a finger over a smear of lip gloss beneath my lip, before turning and opening the door. I wish I hadn't, though.

Anger radiates off him like hot rays of the sun, burning my skin before uttering a single word.

He knows.

"Is there someone else?" he asks, but his attention isn't on me, instead, he looks out over the running creek, just yards from where he's leaning against the railing.

"No, Lance, it's not like that," I reply, stepping out onto the porch, but keeping my distance.

"Why don't you tell me what it is like then, Harlyn, because I thought we had something. Why are you suddenly sidestepping and giving up on us? Is it because I don't come from the kind of money the rest of you people do?"

The urge to remind him things ended months ago is right on the tip of my tongue, but I refrain when I realize what he's said. After all this time, his assumption about me being so shallow and the reason for our breakup being money or status, sets me off. I move into his line of sight and glare at him. "Lance, you know money was never the issue. It's just...we don't see eye to eye on anything."

"I didn't hear any complaints in the bedroom," he remarks flatly.

"Sex alone isn't going to hold this relationship together. I like you for you, not your money or how good in bed you are, but I don't think that's enough, do you? Aren't you looking for someone who will love you with all their heart, not just like?" I ask, placing a palm on his cheek.

He lets out a deep breath. "I disagree. There's something more but I think you're not willing to admit it." He takes my chin between his thumb and forefinger. "I'll make you see it one way or another, Harlyn."

Without so much as a second glance, he turns on his heel and heads back down the drive before straddling his motorcycle and driving off.

I'm left standing there alone, and confused. Was this a breakup, or have I just raised a challenge with a man who doesn't hold my heart?

Chapter 4

Francis Harlyn Aldridge

THE NEXT MORNING, MY mind is still reeling from the conversation with Lance. His inability to understand we're over is partly my fault. I've been weak and have given in when tempted with sex or just an offer of spending time together. But that ends now. Today is a new day, and I'm prepared to hold my ground.

My phone chimes, halting my thoughts.

Quinn: Yo, everything okay this morning?

I'd called Quinn last night after Lance had left. She listened to me wallowing in self-pity while the tears flowed for hours, before stepping in and offering her advice. She didn't hold back, either.

"Don't beat yourself up about it, Har. If you weren't feeling it with him, then what you did needed to be done. He thinks he loved you, but I didn't see it. Maybe the conversation about money signals to something about your relationship and his intentions. Could it be he is after yours?"

She'd raised a valid point. There were many occasions where he'd pried a little too deep into detail around my grandfather's will. The thought lingers in the back of my mind. I'd call her and talk through this newly discovered theory, but I'm already running late, so a quick text reply is all I have time for while readying myself for school.

Me: I'm fine. See you in class.

With our schedules not aligned for senior-year, I'll not see her until Mr. Harrington's class, which I'll be late for because I've misplaced my copy of Hamlet again. I was sure I tucked it in my bag to read last night.

I toss things from inside my locker onto the floor, frantically searching for it. There's math, science, and biology textbooks, along with a ton of unnecessary other crap, but no worn hardback.

"Well, it seems I've missed locker cleaning day, ladies," Catarina comments, and giggles erupt around her from what I can only assume are Rebecca and Scarlett—her minions.

Ignoring her, I continue digging through my locker.

"You know it's obvious, don't you?"

I release a frustrated breath and sit back on my heels. She's baiting me; I shouldn't respond, but I'm curious what she feels she needs to point out. "What is so obvious, Catarina?"

"Your crush on Mr. Harrington. Everyone in class sees it. I must say, he would be a step up from that trailer trash scum, Lance Freeman. What I'm curious about, though, is if not having parents at home made you more of a slut than if they were around." More laughter rolls around her.

It's the last straw for me. I stand up and crowd her until I'm in her face. "Don't you dare say anything about my parents, *Rina*," I emphasize the name her friends call her, knowing full-well I'm not one of them.

"Or else, what?" she asks, standing taller.

"You'll regret it," I say, poking her in the collarbone with my finger.

She scoffs at my response and opens her mouth to say something, but the bell rings, signaling we're late. With one flippant glance, she turns on her heel and heads to his classroom. "Let's go, girls. Mr. Harrington is probably waiting for us."

The entire scene makes my blood boil. I've had just about as much as I can take from them. I could've easily unleashed my fists on her if not for the bell. Tossing everything back in my locker, I shove the door close, but it springs open. It takes several shoves before the latch engages, making me even later to class.

Outside Mr. Harrington's classroom, I take a deep breath and prepare myself for what I expect is going to be a disaster, before stepping through the door. Everyone already has their nose in their books, and I breathe a sigh of relief that no one is watching when I enter, but my relief doesn't last.

"Glad you could join us, Miss Aldridge." Announcing my arrival, Mr. Harrington decides to make an example of me.

Giggles and laughs rumble through the classroom, but I ignore them, and instead, saunter to my desk as though my presence is a privilege before taking a seat. "I'm happy to be here, Mr. Harrington," I retort.

The giggles and laughs turn to oohs and a dramatic "burn" from some boys in the back. It draws a narrowed stare from the teacher, but he's quick to regain his composure, and begins his class as though nothing has happened.

"With a show of hands, how many of you finished reading Hamlet last night?" he asks, rising to his feet and coming around to the sit on the front edge of his desk.

There are only a few who don't raise their hand, including me.

"For those of you who've read, I'm going to pass out a quiz. Once you've completed it, place it on my desk quietly, and you're free to go early." The room erupts in whistles and claps from the majority, but a raise of his hand quiets them.

My breath catches when I realize what he's holding. It's my copy of Hamlet. I know it's mine by the pink frilly bookmark, dangling from the top. How did he get it?

Most of the class has e-readers for their required reads, but I still prefer a hardback. There's nothing like the feel and smell of an aged book, especially the older editions like the one he holds so carefully now. That edition was obtained from our home library and is one of the initially published copies, not something you can easily buy off the internet.

"For those of you who haven't finished, please continue reading through the rest of the scenes. If you finish in time, you will be given the quiz and will be able to leave once you've completed it. For those of you who don't finish reading"—his stare lands on me—"I'll give you until Thursday at the latest to have read and completed your quiz. And make sure you do, because coming Friday, I have a surprise announcement. Trust me, you don't want to miss this, so get everything done in time."

More claps and whistles erupt but fade just as quickly when Mr. Harrington begins to hand out quizzes.

When he's handed out all but one, he stalks over to my desk and leans down, handing me my book. "If leaving this in my classroom is some kind of rebellious act, then it just means you'll be spending more time with me."

Fuck. I glance around to see who might be listening, but everyone seems to be reading or completing their work, and I release a sigh. "Thank you," I tell him, reaching for the small book. "I'm sure my parents wouldn't be happy if I were to lose it."

Pulling his arm back, his brows furrow in what appears as confusion. "This wasn't some ploy to get out of schoolwork?"

"What?" I ask a little too loudly, and some of my classmates shush me. I ignore them, turning a stern gaze on the teacher, offended he'd even consider I'd do something like that. "No, of course not."

His body relaxes as though me trying to get out of schoolwork was such a burden for him. He thumbs through the pages and says, "This is a five-thousand-dollar book. I'd expect you'd get in quite some trouble if it were lost. You may want to consider an e-book for the rest of the class."

His knowledge of the book's value doesn't surprise me as an English teacher, but the way he appreciates holding something so valuable in his hand, like it's worth its weight in gold, says a lot about him.

My parents could drop five-grand in an hour without a second thought, and they wouldn't give a shit about this book. Not like I do, and most definitely not the way Mr. Harrington does.

He returns it to me and I grip the edge, but he doesn't let go. Our eyes lock. Everything around me goes silent; papers rustling, the low chatter of students exiting the room as they finish their quizzes, and even the appreciative stare I'm getting from Quinn, all of it moves to the back of my mind.

In my world, at this very moment, it's only Mr. Harrington and me.

Chapter 5

Winston Asher Harrington III

NEVER HAS A STUDENT made me react the way I am now. Her brown eyes peer into my very soul, leaving me feeling vulnerable and speechless. Tutoring her is going to be a challenge for that very reason. I'm not sure why I'd even suggested it. I could take the money her parents offered, but that's not ethical, and I don't need the money.

I genuinely feel this young woman has talent, but there's a strong possibility someone like her, a Society child, would never need anything I can teach, other than forcing her to work hard and earn her grade.

Releasing the book, I give her one last reminder. "Don't forget, our first session is after today's class."

Her lips part as if she's about to say something, but she must have changed her mind, and nods, instead. I acknowledge her by tapping her desk with my fingers, then head back to the front of the class, where I can hide my traitorous dick behind my desk before anyone notices her effect on me.

The rest of the class time goes by quickly.

On occasion, I'd chance a glance at Harlyn, telling myself it was to make sure she was reading, but deep down, I know it's more than that. There's something about her pulling me in. Something different, I just can't put my finger on it. Which is fine because I surely wouldn't use just *one* on her.

Yesterday, when I'd dropped the tutoring suggestion, and she'd called me sir, I was sure my composure would be lost. The innocent way it had rolled off her lips sent an alert signal straight to my dick along with images—I should never have about any of my students—rolling through my mind.

I'm not into hard-core BDSM, or anything even at the intermediate level, but I've dabbled a little and enjoy watching. Her use of the title set off desires I hadn't realized were lurking just below the surface in the back of my mind. It makes me wonder if I should reconsider tutoring her. No, I'm a professional. I've been dealing with students for four years. Some of whom have been incredibly attractive and aggressively interested, but I was able to resist their advances. I can surely control myself around an introvert such as Harlyn.

The afternoon bell buzzes, pulling my attention from my thoughts, and I notice I've been staring at her the entire time. Luckily, the classroom is almost empty. The only stragglers are students who were still reading, but now closing up their books and gathering their things to leave.

Quinn leans in and says something to Harlyn that makes her cheeks tint before she picks up her things and saunters past my desk.

Hmm, seeing her blush like that is forming all kinds of ideas in my mind. Like having her strip down to only her bra and that school issued pleated skirt right here in the classroom. Once her cheeks are the perfect shade of red, I'd bend her over the desk, flip her skirt up, and smack her ass until her bottom cheeks were the same color. Fuck! Asher, get your fucking mind out of the gutter. She's your student.

"Have a good evening, Winston," Quinn says, pulling my attention away from Harlyn and on to her knowing grin before she exits my classroom.

I rub a hand through my hair, hoping it serves as a distraction from the inappropriate thoughts playing in my mind. When I finally focus toward the back there's only Harlyn and I left.

We exchange glances, and damn if those brown eyes don't cause an unwanted twitch between my legs. If I have any plans of getting through the next two weeks without jacking off at the end of every night, then I need to at least try and keep my physical reaction under control. Closing my eyes for a moment, I allow thoughts of scenes from Hamlet to drift through my mind, hoping it'll slow the adrenaline coursing through me. Only when I feel it working do I rise from my seat and move around to the front of my desk. "Before we get started, I want to make sure we agree on the rules of how this will work."

"Okay," she says, her voice a mere whisper and barely audible. "Can I ask a question first?"

"Sure," I reply cautiously, wondering what her question could be.

"Is there any way we could do this in say a setting that is, not the school?"

With furrowed brows my thoughts dip into the gutter again. Is she asking because she's having feelings, too? Maybe she wants to meet somewhere a little less formal. No, I'm reading too much into it. "It depends on what are your reasons are."

She exhales a heavy breath. "I just don't want anyone from class to know I'm being tutored. You don't know how hard it is when they tease. It's very emotionally draining and would distract me from my studies. Popularity is everything here at Silvercrest High, Mr. Harrington. One negative comment from someone as popular as Catarina, and I might as well switch schools."

It had never actually occurred to me she might face a rath from the other students if they knew. And there's no fucking way I'm letting her leave. Swallowing down a knot of anger formed by the thought of how cruel high school kids can be, I try and ease her concerns. "Hmm, let me give it some thought. For today, let's just work through the lesson I'd planned, and tomorrow, we can decide what venue might work for the rest of the sessions. Deal?"

"Deal." Her face beams at my proposal.

That expression is something I'd love to see daily, and while I don't want that smile to disappear, I know she needs to understand the rules. "Okay, so this is how it'll work from now on. Every day, after class, you and I will meet for an hour. There will be no exceptions for absence, Harlyn. If you're going to be late or you can't make it due to unforeseen circumstances, you must let me know beforehand, and they must be dire. Understand?"

"Circumstances must be dire. Got it." She huffs out.

"You'll have homework. I expect it to be completed by the next day if we don't finish in class. And lastly, I expect you to put in an effort. I'm taking time out of my afternoon to help you. If you're not planning on trying, then there's the door. Just know, walking out is an automatic D grade. Do you agree with these terms, Miss Aldridge?"

She looks to the door as though she's contemplating leaving, but instead she opens her book, and lifts her eyes to mine. "Yes, I agree. Where do we start?"

"That's my girl," I praise, but instantly regret it when her eyes widen, and a gasp forces her lips apart, drawing my attention to the full pink flesh. The thought of covering her mouth with mine has my dick stirring in my pants. But no matter how tempting she is we have work to do. Clearing my throat, I lift my eyes to hers and redirect my focus on what she's here for. "How about we start with the last scene you read?"

"Okay, I believe it was Act IV, scene V." She opens the book to where the bookmark holds her place.

I stalk over to her desk, intent on confirming the page with her but instead my thoughts sway to everything that is Harlyn. From the chocolate brown orbs teasing my soul as they dance between mine, to those sweetheart shaped lips that don't touch completely when her mouth is closed, I can't resist any longer. I take her dainty chin in my palm and lean in until I'm only a breath away. "I want to taste you, Harlyn."

She shivers under my ministrations, and her eyes flutter closed.

Her answer is clear, but I need to hear her say it. "Dammit Harlyn, tell me to stop. Tell me you don't want this."

"I can't," she whispers huskily, before wrapping an arm around my neck and pulling me against her.

Shock is what registers in my mind first. The way she takes control unsettles me, throwing me off my game, but only for a moment. Once her tongue glides over my bottom lip, my fingers tangle in her hair, and I take the lead. Devouring her mouth like a man on death row, eating his last meal.

At this moment, no one else exists. The school, my family, this town, everything around me fades into oblivion. It's only Harlyn and I. A forbidden pair coming together without regard for the consequences.

The afternoon bell rings and it's like an electric shock, breaking our connection. Breathing heavily, I drop my forehead to hers. "Maybe you can read the rest at home."

She nods but doesn't say another word before pulling away and gathering her things. It's as though she's ashamed of what she's done. I can't let her leave like this. "Harlyn, are you okay?"

Ignoring me, she stands up and prepares to move toward the door.

"Look at me," I command, gripping her arm, keeping her from leaving. My breath catches at what I see when she does. A single tear has escaped down her cheek, and I fear I've hurt her somehow. Pulling her against me, she drops her books to the floor and wraps her arms around me, sobbing into my shirt.

I smooth a hand over the back of her head and soothe her, while she releases whatever it is she's feeling. The fact she doesn't resist and is still in my arms, letting go of whatever this is, tells me it's not because of what we've just done. This is something bigger. Something that has been bottled up inside for quite some time.

I am disheartened at the fact no one saw this coming, yet honored that she chose me to expose this side of herself.

"I-I'm s-sorry," she stutters, her voice cracking through sobs.

"Shhh, it's okay. Let it out. Get it all out."

When her sobs begin to wane, she leans back and plucks at my wet, wrinkled shirt. "I'm really am sorry. Is it ruined?"

I glance down at where her hands rest, chuckling softly. "No, sweetheart. And even if it were, I wouldn't care," I assure her while wrapping my arms around her waist and placing a kiss on her cheek. "Do you want to talk about it?"

Her red-rimmed eyes lift to mine and it feels like forever before she answers. I imagine she's debating on if she can trust me. She can, no matter what it is, but I can't make that decision for her, so I remain quiet.

"Rain check? I'm not sure I'm quite ready yet." She shrugs, swiping tears from her cheek.

"You know where to find me."

Her lips twist up in a small smile before she pulls away and begins gathering her things once again then heads toward the door, pausing only long enough to give me one last needy glance before she steps through.

The breath I was holding finally escapes and I drop to a nearby desk. What in the fuck have I just done? "So much for self-control, Asher," I reprimand myself, scrubbing a hand over my face before lowering my eyes to where she'd just been sitting. That's when I see it.

Her copy of Hamlet.

Is it an invitation, maybe to drop by her home?

Or did she truly forget?

If it's the latter, I may lift that skirt of hers after all.

Chapter 6

Winston Asher Harrington III

I'D NEVER RETURNED the book to her last night. Instead, I wanted to see her reaction after not having it all evening. And I'm not disappointed. After digging through her book bag for several minutes I feel bad and approach her desk. Leaning close to her ear. "You really should be more careful with this."

She nods, brushing my hand with hers as she takes back the classic but doesn't lift her head. I want to grip her chin and make her turn those big brown eyes on me but I'm not risking her reputation or my career and instead I head back up to the front of the room. Taking a seat and watching her read page after page of a play I know she's not into.

It gives me some time to think about her question. The one about moving our tutoring sessions.

Five minutes is all it takes to realize the perfect place, and when I do, I practically fling myself out of my chair. I know I can't tell her now, so instead, I pace about in front of the classroom before leaning against the front of my desk, waiting until the final bell rings and the classroom is clear.

She eyes the door cautiously, what with the last student having left just moments ago but I can't resist having her against me and when she approaches, I wrap my fingers around her arm and pull her between my legs. Not wasting any time giving her the good news between kisses. "We're... meeting ...at... the... library."

"The library. Got it, now stop," she giggles as my five o'clock shadow tickles her face. "otherwise, we're going to get caught."

I'm disappointed at the absence of her warmth when she pushes off me to retrieve her book bag. But she makes up for it with one small kiss on my lips, before turning her back on me and disappearing through the door.

The rest of my time is spent in an empty classroom clearing my desk off before it's time to see her again. And the way I'm feeling now, the hands on the clock can't move fast enough.

THE BUILDING IS RIGHT on the outskirts of town, and was built in honor of the Harrington family in the early 1900s. Teaching The Society children has been the role of women in the Harrington family for generations. I'm the exception.

I wasn't interested in the family real estate business and had my heart set on filling the minds of others with knowledge, but my father disapproved. No son of his would ever stand in front of a class, teaching a room full of snot-nosed, overly privileged children. "I'm one of those over-privileged kids, Dad," I'd told him, and it had earned me a slap on the face. He essentially forced my hand into his business by threatening my cash flow. If I pursued teaching, my funds would be cut off.

Fortunately for me, he died. My mother recognized how miserable I was and made sure I got what I needed to become who I am today—a male teacher, who at this moment, is heading to give yet another student his undivided attention. Hopefully, I can push aside thoughts of her tiny body in that school uniform and keep my dick under control.

When I arrive, I park in the Reserved – Harrington Family parking spot, and head inside.

The interior is what you'd expect from a library. The scent of pages covered in words permeates the air around me, while overwhelming rows of books after books are stacked neatly all throughout the room.

What's unique about the large space are the public rooms offset from the main book area, where visitors can meet or simply enjoy some privacy. I have chosen a secluded place for Harlyn and me. Not only will it squash her fears of being seen by any classmates but also reduce any distractions.

"Hi Mr. Harrington," our resident librarian greets.

"Tasha." I offer her a nod and then realize I'm not sure where I'm going. "Can you point me in the direction of the Mesa Verde room? It's been some time since I've been here."

"Sure, Mr. Harrington, this way," she guides me down a short hall, before turning a corner and stopping just short of a dead end.

Standing in front of the Mesa Verde room, I notice the door is ajar, and I peek through the glass. There sits Harlyn, wringing her fingers and squirming in her seat. The determination I had about refraining from any sexual thoughts flutter right out of my mind with one glance.

"Anything else, Mr. Harrington?"

"No, thanks, Tasha. I've got it from here," I say, not looking back at her because all my focus is on the girl, waiting nervously on the other side.

It's times like these I wonder if I should've listened to my father and stuck with real estate. If I'd met Harlyn while showing a house, at a coffee shop, or anywhere else, at least then, the thoughts I've been having wouldn't be inappropriate, and potentially risky enough to cost my job. I just need to get through this week.

I step through the door, and her eyes lift up to meet mine. I offer her a smile, and it seems to relax her because she offers her own in return.

"Harlyn, I want to apologize for what happened yesterday—"

With a raised hand, she stops me. "You don't need to apologize. You didn't do anything I didn't want. But this isn't how I want to get my grade, Mr. Harrington. I want to earn it. I know I can."

She's saying everything I want to hear, including her earning her grade. But as great as that sounds I can't prevent my mind from drifting to how she could do that on her knees. I am a man after all. Maybe if I taped pages of literature across my stomach… the thought brings a chuckle from deep in my chest that I mask with a cough. "It's interesting you say that since I found this, on your desk yesterday."

Her smile widens and somehow turns mischievous. "That's for you."

"What do you mean it's for me?"

She raises her e-reader and shows me her copy of Hamlet before nodding back to the book in my hand. "Go on, open it."

Just on the inside of the cover is a folded note. I glance back to her, and she nods. Cautiously, I unfold the paper and read the contents aloud.

Mr. Harrington,

I could see your appreciation for books goes beyond that of even a collector. No one has ever shown an interest in helping me achieve anything, and for that, I'm incredibly grateful. Please accept this $5847 copy of Hamlet as a way of showing my appreciation.

Sincerely,

Francis Harlyn Aldridge.

My chest tightens as I read through the note again this time to myself. It's heartfelt and sincere just like her signature says. Coming from someone that doesn't want for anything, I'm overwhelmed by her generosity. Suddenly, my earlier needs take a backseat to the worn book in my hand. I extend it out to her. "Harlyn, this is probably the most thoughtful thing anyone has ever done for me. And as much as I appreciate this amazing gift, I can't accept it."

She stands up and comes around the table, pushing the book and my hands against my chest. "You can, and you will," she says. "Please, let me just do this for you."

I place the book on the table behind us, and pull her against me. "Thank you." Is all I manage to get out before my lips crash down on hers.

All it took is just one taste, and now I can't get enough. Her presence alone makes my mind and my body weak. If we don't stop this now, there's no telling how it might end up.

I reluctantly pull away.

She touches her lips as though the assault was too much, but then she smiles. "That's the best thank you I've ever gotten."

I offer her a grin back and then smack her on the ass. "Take a seat and let's get started. I'm not teaching sex ed, you know."

"Oh? Then I guess I'm in the wrong class." She readies herself to leave but it's too late her teasing has already ignited a fire in my veins.

"Sit, Harlyn."

Sauntering over to the opposite side of the table she pushes out that bottom lip, and with the most seductive stare I've ever seen, says, "Yes, sir." Before dropping into the seat.

"I'm warning you. We're here to study, and if you keep pushing that lip out and saying *sir,* I'm going to turn you over this table, and—"

"—and what, Mr. Harrington, shove your dick in my ass?" She slaps a hand over her mouth and her eyes go wide as though shocked by her own words.

My breath catches, and I swallow deep. I'm on a very thin edge of saying fuck it and indulging both of us, but giving in wouldn't give what either of us needs. Well, not on a literary level, anyway.

"How about this? You get through today, and by the end of the week, produce a quiz with ninety-eight percent or better, and I'll stick this dick wherever you want it." I take her hand and place it on the bulge in my pants, proving my point.

My dick is one hell of a motivator because she powers up her reading device and goes straight to the last page she was on, taking notes as she quickly scans the pages.

"Ninety-eight percent or better, remember?"

She nods frantically and continues reading at a record pace.

Chapter 7

Francis Harlyn Aldridge

THIS MORNING, I'M SKIPPING class and going dress shopping with Quinn. There's a charity ball organized by the Mayor in just a few days, and I haven't bought anything to wear. I assume getting my size might be a challenge because, according to Quinn's mom, I don't care how much I weigh. I wanted to bitch-slap her for even insinuating I'm overweight, but I held my tongue, brushing it off as if I didn't hear her.

Hell, I'm a size four. If having curves in all the right places is a sin, I guess I'll be dancing with the devil.

The more I think about the ball, the more I wonder if spending money on a dress is necessary. After my conversation with Lance a couple of days ago, I doubt our plans to go together are still on the table.

It's not like I need a date. The money my absentee parents donated will be enough to guarantee me a seat at any table, but I'd be going with Mr. Harrington if I had my way. And not because being near him gets my panties wet, but also because I'd love to see the looks on all the rich bitches' faces when I'd walk in on the teacher's arm.

Neither Quinn nor I consume the coffee or muffins I'd so graciously brought. Her mother had set me on edge, and there's no way I'm trying on dresses after bloating from a bunch of carbs.

There are many dress shops in Silvercrest, but everyone knows, showing up at a ball in a dress bought anywhere but Vinnik's is essentially your ticket out of elite status.

Known for unique, original, and one of a kind styles by the most famous designers from all over the world is what you'll find there, and it's where Quinn and I are now.

It wasn't, but ten minutes after I stepped through the door, I found the dress I'm wearing.

The strapless deep-cut V neck bodice is dark navy, flattering my breasts and hips as it angles into a matching V shape at my waist. From there, waves of sapphire silk is meticulously hand-sewn into the dark navy that eventually extends into a floor-length flowing skirt. It's elegant yet sexy and totally me. I'm ecstatic when I learn it's a size four.

Quinn isn't as lucky. The lack of her boyfriend's response to numerous texts that include pictures of her first choice puts her in a mood, and she dumps the dress on a neatly folded pile of lingerie before stalking off to another part of the shop, ultimately settling on a sexy black and red gown.

She arranges alterations with the women behind the counter, and shortly after we disappear through the door.

"Harlyn, what are you doing today? Are you hooking up with Winston later?"

She's trying to bait me into giving her more information on the teacher but to her surprise my response is only a shrug. I still haven't told her or anyone for that matter, about mine and Mr. Harrington's arrangement. It's not that I don't trust her since we're both a part of The Society, and have learned the value of loyalty from a young age. Those who are not loyal, generally don't live to tell their tale. But, in this case, it's personal.

Yeah, it's only a tutoring session, but the attraction between Winston and I is indescribable. Every time we see one another, it becomes more profound, and I feel it's only a matter of time before we lose ourselves in intimacy. So, for now, I'm keeping this to myself.

When she pulls into my drive, we say our goodbyes, and I step out of the car where Anderson, my butler, is waiting on the stairs. I'd texted him moments ago, letting him know I'd be heading home after shopping, and he should be ready for my bags.

Once in my room, I drop onto the bed and watch the hours tick by before meeting with Mr. Harrington.

"I've hung your dress in the guest room, Miss Aldridge," Anderson says from outside my room.

"Thank you." I shout toward the door, hopeful he can hear me because I'm not moving off this bed until I have to.

Once the shuffle of his feet disappears down the hall and I know he's gone, I turn over on my side and scroll through social media on my phone, but it doesn't hold my attention. Instead, my thoughts begin drifting to the man I'll be seeing later. Wondering what he'll be wearing and how he'll smell. Will I get close enough to touch him, maybe even kiss him again? My heart pounds quickly in my chest and I consider slipping my hand inside my panties. If anything, getting myself off would lessen my nerves while I'm around him.

After a beat I decide against it because I can't avoid the desire to see him any longer. Hopping off the bed and skipping down the stairs, I burst through the front door, heading to meet a teacher I have no business being around in my current state of mind.

With each mile, my heart rate increases, as do my feelings for him. I've never felt this way with Lance or any of the other boys I've dated. The excitement of knowing I'll feel the teacher's lips against mine once again sends an undeniable need straight to the space between my legs.

It's a dangerous line we're treading on. A teacher-student relationship is not something well received in the town of Silvercrest, or being a child of The Society. I might as well prepare for a target on my back.

But I'm willing to take that risk. I only hope it's worth it in the end.

Chapter 8

Winston Asher Harrington III

HARLYN MISSED CLASS today, but she'd done as I asked and texted, letting me know she'd be out. The reason wasn't something I'd consider dire as we'd discussed, but since she's still meeting me for her tutoring session, I've decided not to adjust her grade because of it.

As I sit in the Mesa Verde room waiting, I think about how mundane class was without her in it. There were no opportunities to glance at her flirty brown eyes or that pouty bottom lip. Instead, I'd had to sit through an hour of Catarina knowing the answer to every question and then some.

The door across from me opens, drawing my attention from my thoughts of class and back to the present. I know I should stand as any gentleman would but by staying seated, she's unaware of the predicament rising in my pants once she steps fully into the room.

In an instant her eyes find mine, and her face brightens with a smile. She doesn't say anything as she dumps her books on the floor, stalks around the table, and straddles my lap, before taking my face in her hands. No words are spoken and without any hesitation her lips cover mine, moving furiously as she takes what she wants.

At first, I'm taken a bit by surprise, but it doesn't take long to synchronize with her. When I adjust my seat in the chair and pull her closer, a gasp escapes against my lips, telling me she's realized my situation, but it doesn't stop her assault on my mouth.

With her school uniform on, the only thing separating us is my jeans and her panties. Her heat warms my cock, and I'm on the brink of losing my load as I wrap an arm around her back, holding her in place while our tongues dance together.

After a beat, she pulls away, breathing heavily. "Take me, Mr. Harrington."

Her respectful use of my surname reminds me what we're doing is wrong, and I consider stopping this, but the thought flits from my mind as quickly as it came when she squirms in my lap. "Asher," I instruct.

"Hmmm?" She cocks her head with hooded eyes.

"My name, it's Asher. Call me Asher, otherwise, we'll need to stop."

When she leans back, her stare bounces between mine; it's as though she's deciding if Asher is who she wants. All this time, I've been Mr. Harrington to her, and at this very moment, we've reached a crossroad.

One direction leads us back to safety, back to a teacher and a student. The other...well, it takes us into new a whole new territory—a place where, if we're not careful, someone will most certainly get hurt.

Even with our clothing separating us, the urge to press my cock against her warm pussy is eating me alive, but I know if I do, it could manipulate her decision, so I wait.

With one final kiss to my lips, she pulls back and looks me straight in the eyes. "Asher, please. Take me right here, right now, in the Mesa Verde room of the Harrington library."

The sound of our family name rolling off her lips is like a song. A beautiful ballad, sung from the voice of an angel. My willpower dissipates into thin air, and my fingers fumble with the buckle of my pants.

She's already removed her shirt over her head and has scooted back, brushing my hands away so she can unfasten the belt and the button, before unzipping my jeans.

Her movements are of someone who's done this before. Not quite an expert, but also not inexperienced.

Once she's exposed my briefs, her hand dips beneath the waistband, and her fingers wrap around my cock, pulling it free. She pauses for a moment, glancing downward, taking in my size, before her eyes lift to mine and God help me, she smiles.

From there, everything is in what feels like a slow-motion film.

Standing up just enough to pull her panties aside and line up the head of my cock with her opening, she begins to lower herself. It's not until she's entirely seated and rotating her hips on me, I realize I'm not wearing a condom. I want to stop her; I need to stop, but her tight pussy is disintegrating every thought in my head, and what happens next is pure animalistic.

Gripping her shoulders, I take control. Sliding in and out of her, slow at first forcing her moans until I can't take it any longer and I pound out a rhythmic pace until she's arching her back and crying out her release.

It's a beautiful sight, watching a woman orgasm. An emotion so raw and vulnerable as it passes over their face, giving men a feeling of power, maybe even control, but in reality, we know they hold all the control. As she is now when her pussy contracts, over and over again, milking me until my release fills her with the Harrington seed.

Once the pounding in my chest has subsided some, I guide her lips to mine for one last kiss before she lays her head on my shoulder, and I lower my arms to around her waist.

We sit quietly, still connected, until our breathing calms.

Having her body on me is both comforting and torture. My dick twitches as she squirms in my lap. I fear it's not long before I'm ready to go again, but as much as I'd like to stay in this position the rest of the day, fucking her in the Harrington library, it's only a matter of time before we get caught. And we need to talk about the fact I didn't use a condom.

Directing her eyes to mine, I start the dreaded conversation, "Harlyn, we need to..." Something flashes past the window by the door, interrupting my thought. I didn't catch it at first, but my eyes are now focused on the transparent glass as I watch for it again.

"Need to what?" she asks lazily.

I don't answer.

I'm rendered speechless.

There, on the other side of the window, is Catarina.

She can't see our connection beneath the table, but in Harlyn's shirtless state and our current position gives away our intimate relationship.

Her mouth is open in what I can only assume is shock, but it doesn't last because, after a beat, her lips turn up in a mischievous grin.

This is not good. I could lose my job and possibly risk never working as a teacher again, but that I can deal with. I'm more worried about what this could do for the last few weeks of Harlyn's senior year and beyond.

Teenagers can be cruel. Add to that a small town, and the peaceful life she deserves will ultimately be turned upside down.

Somehow, I need to fix this.

Harlyn turns her head, trying to follow my gaze, but I'm quick to take her head in my hands and focus her attention on me. The less she knows, the better. "We need to talk about how much I enjoyed what we've just done." It's not the whole truth, since I'd wanted to talk with her about the condom, or lack thereof. But that can wait. The chances of any fallout from what we've done are low.

"Hmm, me too."

"How about you go get cleaned up, and we can finish, or should I say start your lesson?"

She giggles at my slip of the tongue, then raises enough to kiss me before slipping on her shirt, grabbing her purse and exiting through the door. I'm hopeful Catarina isn't hiding on the other side.

When there's no noise coming from the hall, I can only assume it means we're safe, but who knows for how long.

Chapter 9

Francis Harlyn Aldridge

RETURNING FROM THE restroom, I noticed a change in Asher's mood. Assuming it was because of the fact we'd had unprotected sex, I assured him I was on birth control and that there were no concerns medically.

He'd apologized for the same, but then, he sat me down and began explaining how irresponsible us having sex in the library was and that it can't happen again. I didn't need a lecture; in fact, I'd do it again in a heartbeat—it was hot as fuck.

We never did finish my lesson. With his mind elsewhere he'd decided it best we call it a night. We'd pick it up where we left off, the next day.

Once we'd said our goodbyes, he walked me to my car without a lingering glance. In fact, he'd been looking over his shoulder and watching everyone but me. "Are you looking for your next target?" I ask jokingly.

His eyes dart to mine, and his brows raise. "What? No. Why would you ask that?"

"Well, maybe because you haven't looked me in the eye since we left the library. Was I not, you know, any good?"

"Oh, Harlyn..." he says, his expression soft, as he grips my arm and pulls me between two massive black SUVs, before backing me against one of them with his body. "You were amazing. I'm just cautious because if we get caught, whatever this is will be over before it even starts." He tips up my chin with a finger. "We just need to be careful."

I nod my agreement and move to place a kiss on his lips, but he pulls away.

On a huff, I tell him, "I understand, Asher. We need to be careful. Now, would you kiss me already?"

My wish is his command. He lowers his lips onto mine, and we become lost in a moment of pleasure; until he pulls away, swats me on the ass, and says, "Now get out of here. I believe you have some homework to do."

I laugh at his playfulness and head to my car.

The drive home is uneventful, and the sky is dark by the time I arrive, but you wouldn't know by how the exterior of the massive three-story antebellum home is lit up. My parents feel the added lights are for safety. I feel like it's a nuisance.

Nevertheless, it's what I call home, and right at this moment, I'm ready to sink beneath the layers of bubbles in a hot bath.

As I step through the massive carved pine entry doors, Anderson greets me in the foyer and takes my book bags from me. "Good evening, Miss Harlyn. Did everything go okay with your lesson this afternoon?"

I can't help the heat that tints my cheeks, remembering just how well it went. "Yes, everything went fine, Anderson. Please have Grace run me a hot bubble bath. I'm going to grab a quick bite from the kitchen," I inform him.

"Will do, Miss Harlyn. There is a plate of food already arranged for you in the refrigerator if you'd like," he calls, but I'm already down the hall. I toss him a wave back instead of shouting my thanks across the house.

Once I'm out of the bath, dried and tucked up in my bed, today's images roll around in my head. It reminds me of how he felt inside. Much larger than I'd expected, it had been painful at first, but didn't take long for me to adjust. The thoughts send a twinge of need to my pussy, and I consider reaching beneath the sheets, but refrain myself from doing so. I'd rather wait until our next time together, instead of marring the memory of our time today.

At that, I turn over in bed and quickly drift off to sleep.

THE ANNOYING BUZZ OF my alarm pulls me from a deep slumber, and after banging on it to stop, I move slowly from the bed.

Usually, I'd be excited tomorrow is the weekend, but that means not having a reason to see Asher for two full days. I suppose there's a small chance he'll be at the masquerade ball tomorrow night. Not that we'll be together, but I'll at least be able to see him. It reminds me I still need to cancel the arrangements with Lance. I tap his face on the screen of my phone.

He answers on the first ring, "Hey babe, how are you this morning?"

My eyes roll at his term of endearment. He is making this a difficult conversation to have, I can already tell. "Hey Lance. I know we haven't discussed this yet, and I'm sorry for the short notice, but I wanted to let you know Anderson will be driving me to the charity ball tomorrow night."

"Your butler? You're having the butler take you to the ball?" he questions, his tone rising in an octave with each word.

"He's not taking me; he's driving me there and dropping me off."

"No, Harlyn. You're not going to the ball alone. I know you think we're on some kind of break, but as I said, I'm not giving up that easily. My tuxedo, the seats at the table, everything has been arranged already. You and I are still going—together."

He's partly right. If I show up to the ball alone, I might as well kiss my social status goodbye. Yeah, I'm a Society kid, but it doesn't guarantee my future as a socialite. Showing up at a ball with no man on my arm will show how insignificant and unwanted I am. I'd have to work that much harder to build myself back up in their eyes.

"Fine, we can go together—as friends, nothing more. Got it?" I huff out.

"I'll pick you up at seven, Harlyn. Be ready." With that, he ends the call.

Our conversation leaves me feeling like I've just made a deal with the devil. Only time will tell if it was the right decision.

Chapter 10

Lance Freeman

HARLYN DOESN'T HAVE any idea, but the charity ball is the perfect place for making an announcement I've wanted to make for some time. I realize it should've come sooner, and I know she's been on the fence about our relationship, but it's unlikely she'll say no in front of all her friends and her family.

A little birdy told me her parents would be returning from their trip early and attending the ball. I'd never have their blessing because I don't come from a Silvercrest founding family, and with being a detective, my values aren't in line with those of The Society, but I don't care what anyone else thinks.

Harlyn is mine. She has been mine even before I arrived back from that torturous boot camp. I'll admit I've made mistakes. Some I'll never recover from, but taking her hand will not be one of them.

I pull the ring from my pocket and stare at the brilliance sparkling back at me. It's not as large as I would've liked, but it was my mother's, and I expect she'll appreciate the sentimental value over what my salary could afford. I give it one last look before tucking it away in a box on top of my dresser.

Once I've dressed and clipped my badge to my belt, I head out the door and climb into an unmarked car.

When the mayor approached me about an opportunity to become a detective after being out of the academy, for only a few months, I jumped at the chance. I didn't understand what the consequences would be at that time. Now that I know, it's too late to get out of it.

Unfortunately, at the center of this master plan is Harlyn and her grandfather's will.

Chapter 11

Francis Harlyn Aldridge

MATH CLASS IS A DRAG today. Well, math is a drag every day, but today is especially heinous. We have a substitute, and their idea of teaching is to write a bunch of problems on the board, and we supply the answers on paper. If he hadn't taken a roll call, I would've never known he even knew how to speak.

I couldn't be more excited to hear the bell ring now than I have all day, since my next class is with Asher.

I don't bother going to my locker between classes, because I want to see him before anyone arrives.

My heart pounds as I quicken my steps toward his door, practically falling in the middle of the hall when I slide to a stop. Taking in a deep breath, I turn the handle and step inside, but what I witness causes me to choke on that same breath.

Asher and Catarina are the only ones in class, and he's leaning over her desk like he's done to me on so many occasions. They're so interested in whatever it is she's saying they don't even notice me walk in.

I've never experienced jealousy at this level before, and I hate it. If it were anyone else in class, I know it wouldn't be a problem, but Catarina? She made a point to mention my crush on Asher. Yet she's still making the moves on him just like the slut that she is.

Well, two can play that game. I drop my books onto my desk and they make a loud thud. It does the trick, drawing their attention to me. "Sorry," I say, narrowing my stare on the woman, taking all the focus of my man.

What I don't expect is the angry expression I get in response from him. "It's okay Catarina, we can go through this after class. I have another student I'm working with, but I can make some adjustments to that schedule," he quips.

At that moment, my heart sinks. Not only did he dismiss me with that face, but he also told her he's working with another student. I mean, how long will it be before she makes the connection that it's me?

Did our time not mean anything yesterday?

Tears tease the corners of my eyes, and I lower my gaze to the open book on my desk. It has nothing to do with this class, but I need the distraction.

When other kids start filing in with their laughter and conversations, I consider ditching the rest of class, but I can guarantee, Mr. Harrington wouldn't allow it. Plus, I'm not someone who gives up that easily. If she thinks she's getting her hands on him, she has another thing coming.

The rest of the class, I follow her lead. Whenever Mr. Harrington asks a question, no matter if I know the answer or not, I raise my hand just as she does. It earns a few chuckles from the class when I get one wrong, but at least I'm trying, or so they think.

I'm relieved when the bell rings finally, but I'm also unsure of what to do next. Usually, I'd head straight over to the library, but if my teacher is going to be helping that bitch, then maybe I'm just supposed to head home.

"Harlyn," he calls out, and once he has my attention, he motions me forward until I'm hovering over his desk. "I'd like to talk to you about this assignment you turned in."

When I glance down, I notice it's not an assignment at all. It's an invitation to our next tutoring session at his home. The thought of meeting him at his home has my heart racing and all kinds of ideas rolling through my head about what we could do other than talking about anything related to school. But then as I read further, the note says tomorrow.

Tomorrow is the charity ball, and I can't miss it.

It also means he'll be spending the rest of this afternoon with her.

I turn and pin a stare on Catarina. She meets my gaze, and her lips turn up in a mischievous grin. This is her way of making a play on him, and I'm not going to let that happen. Swiping a pen from his desk, I write a note on the same invitation. Plans tomorrow, can we meet later tonight?

He looks from Catarina and back to me. There's turmoil in his eyes. It's as though the decision between us is one too difficult to make.

I'm not sure what game this is, but I'm no longer interested in playing. I grab the paper from his desk, wadding it in my palm and tossing it in the trash. It's my fuck-you to him and his invitation.

Chapter 12

Winston Asher Harrington III

IT CRUSHED ME TO SEE Harlyn storm out of class yesterday. The realization of how much my feelings have grown for her over the school year happened at that moment.

After the library, I'd been seriously considering talking with her about a long-term relationship, once she graduates of course, and tonight was supposed to be just that. But she is no longer answering any of my texts.

The situation with Catarina wasn't my idea. It's not something I want to do, but when she came to class early, threatening to expose what she saw at the library, I knew something had to be done. Now she's out of the picture and I can focus my attention on Harlyn, which is why my tux lies on the bed.

I hadn't planned on attending the charity ball, but I'd made a sizable donation, which means they'd have a seat reserved in my honor, whether empty or not.

I know it's a risk confronting her there. This dance is where only the elite come together—members of the school board,

Society members, and just parents in general. There's also the added chance Harlyn won't be there alone.

People talk, and if you're in the right circles, you hear things. I know she and Lance were a thing, and I was glad to learn she ended it. He's a shady bastard and will do whatever it takes to hide the fact his blood is not from a founding family.

I suspect if she's going, it'll be with him.

"There's only one way to find out," I tell myself, sliding from the bed, and head toward the shower.

Once I've dried and dressed, I'm fumbling with my tie when my cell rings. Expecting it's the one I have been dreaming about all day, I answer without looking at the number. "Harlyn?"

"I'd never wish that on my worst enemy," the voice on the other line says.

"Catarina, I thought we had an understanding," I growl.

"Oh, we do, and as I told you, my word is my promise. I'll not say anything to anyone about what I saw in the library, and in return, you owe me private tutoring and one favor." She clears her throat. "I'm calling in that favor."

"Whatever it is, it'll have to wait. I've got plans," I tell her, preparing to end the call.

"I know you're planning on going to the dance; it's the reason for my call. See, my date canceled at the last minute..."

"No! Absolutely not!" I shout. "I will not show up with you, Catarina, even if I wanted to. It's the same reason I hadn't asked Harlyn. I could lose my job."

She releases a frustrated breath. "Just let me worry about that. Pick me up at 7:30 pm. I want to be fashionably late." When the line goes quiet but there's no dial tone, I assume she's waiting for my reply.

The fact I'm even considering this means I've lost my ever-loving mind. I know if I do it, I risk everyone seeing us together, but if I don't, Catarina goes straight to her parents who are on the school board. Balancing which option poses more risk is what I'm considering now. "If I take you, how will you ensure I don't lose my job?"

"If my parents ask, I plan on telling them it's a school project. We're doing an experiment on what it would be like to be socially outcast. I mean, I've never actually been in that position, so it's believable. My parents will inform everyone what we're doing to avoid the shame of their daughter attending a dance with her teacher. Even if I told them not to say anything because it would ruin the whole idea of the project, they would still do it just to avoid any embarrassment."

She makes a good point. It could be a valid project, not that I'd recommend anyone take that risk. Catarina has a confident head on her shoulders, and if anyone can handle the backlash, it would be her. "Fine, I'll meet you in front of your house at 7:15."

Explaining this to Harlyn is not something I'm looking forward to, but she'll understand once she knows everything.

Chapter 13

Francis Harlyn Aldridge

THE CHIME OF THE DOORBELL echoes through the house, and I hear Anderson answer.

"Greetings, Mr. Freeman. Miss Aldridge, is expecting you. Please, come in, and have a seat."

Heels of what I expect are mid-priced dress shoes, click on the marble foyer, and stop at the bottom of the stairs. "There's no time for sitting, Anderson; we're running a bit late. Harlyn, are you ready?" he asks, his deep timber flowing up toward the second floor.

"I'll be right down." My response is shaky as nerves twist my stomach in knots.

I should've pushed harder at going to the party alone. If there's even a slight possibility that Asher will be there, arriving with Lance will put whatever we started in jeopardy.

I have a suspicion this night isn't going to end well.

Taking a deep breath, I rest my hand on the railing and begin my descent down the stairs—the small train of navy-blue silk dragging on each step behind me. When I reach the midway point of the arched staircase, and my gaze meets the raised brows and parted lips of Lance's shocked expression, I know this dress was the right choice.

"Damn, Harlyn, you look amazing."

Lance's words are kind, and I'm appreciative, but in the back of my mind, I wish it were Asher waiting for me at the base of the stairs, and it was him watching me the way Lance is now. "Thank you," I tell him, reaching for his elbow as I take the last step.

Just as we reach the door and are about to step through, Anderson stops us. "Your wrap, Miss. The night might be chilly, and you wouldn't want to be unprotected," he says, directing his attention to Lance.

"Down, boy," Lance retorts before stepping toward my butler and flipping his coat jacket aside, revealing his badge. "Need I remind you I'm a detective, and I can protect Miss Aldridge just fine?"

"No, sir," Anderson replies, standing a bit taller, "It's just a coat, sir,"

My eyes roll at the testosterone-driven verbal battle. If this mild banter is any sign of how the rest of the night will be, then I have nothing to worry about. At least I hope so.

Stepping through the doors, I'm surprised to find a sleek black car awaiting us and not the muscle car Lance is always so proud to flaunt around town. "I thought we'd be riding in the silver bullet."

He chuckles. "Not in that dress, sweetheart. Tonight, I wanted to be the one who treated you like a princess. Plus, if I drove, my eyes would've been on the road and not on you."

I grip his arm stopping him before he reaches for the car door. "Lance, this isn't what you think. I'm going with you as a friend, not your girlfriend. If you can't accept that, then I'll just have Anderson take me." Turning, I prepare to do just that, but he places his hand on my shoulder.

"I understand, Harlyn. I'll try and contain myself. Please, just get in the car. We're already later than I'd expected we'd be."

Glancing from the house to the car, I concede and climb in. He gives no reason for why he's in such a hurry, and I don't ask. I just want to get there, make an appearance, and slip out the back. If we leave early enough, there's still a chance I can take Asher up on his offer of a tutoring session at home.

The ride is filled mostly with idle conversation. It sets my mind at ease, and I relax back in the seat. After what feels like only five minutes later, someone is shaking me. "Har? Harlyn, wake up, we're here."

My lashes flutter until my eyes adjust to the bright white lights strung all about the exterior of the city hall building. How could I have fallen asleep? This is totally unlike me; I'm generally able to survive on only a few hours of sleep.

"Close the door, Danny, we need a moment." Lance tells a figure standing just outside of the car.

Wait, did he just call the driver Danny? "What's going on—" My question is cut off by Lance's hand covering my mouth.

"Before you give me the third degree, let me explain. Okay?" he asks calmly. It's not until I nod my response, he removes his hand. "Good. There's no need to be upset. I know how you feel about Danny, but since I obviously can't afford a limo *and* a driver, he volunteered. I've strictly ordered him to keep his hands off you, both for tonight and any other time."

"Do you think he'll listen? Because we've done this before and at some point, he always reverts to his old ways." I huff, crossing my arms, but quickly set them in my lap when I catch Lance's eyes lowered to my cleavage.

"I told him if he doesn't, I'll shoot him."

I laugh at his response, but stop mid-breath when I realize his response wasn't a joke. "Obviously that's not what I'd want, but Lance, I'm trusting you. One touch or an inappropriate glance and the first call I'll make is to The Society."

"Finally," he says, ignoring my threat and offering me a wink, before grabbing the door handle and exiting the car, then reaching for my hand.

We walk hand-in-arm to the entry doors where Lance hands the doorman our invitations, and he waves us in. Our heels click on the aged marble floor of the city hall's interior as we make our way to the ballroom.

When the double doors open, the room takes my breath away.

Round dining tables are spaced perfectly around the large space, each with meticulous place settings and centerpieces of abstract gold weaved around lit candles: there's a dance floor and a place for a small orchestra each thing adding to the overall ambiance of the room.

Attendees are still gathering, and no one has been seated yet, which means we're right on time. I scan the room for the one person I'm most interested in seeing, but there's no sign of him. I'm both disappointed and relieved.

Lance fidgets nervously at my side.

"Is everything okay?" I ask him.

"Everything's fine," he responds, taking a quick look around. "How about you find our table, and I'll get us some drinks."

Nodding, I head toward the row of tables by the dance floor, glancing back often to see the direction he goes to. Something about him seems off, and I'm not sure what it is. When he walks past the bar and through a small crowd, I forget about finding our table and decide to follow him.

Chapter 14

Lance Freeman

ACCORDING TO DANNY, the one person I wanted here before I make my big announcement hasn't yet arrived, but I needed to get away from Harlyn, otherwise, I would've jumped the gun on asking her.

Right now, I'm just trying to buy some time by doing a quick sweep of the area to see who else I might want to shock with my announcement tonight. I spot Quinn in one of the rooms, but I have no intention of speaking with her. She and I have never gotten along, so she'll have to find out through her friend later.

I'm about to look into another room, when my phone chimes.

Danny: They're parking.

Danny: About three minutes out.

Me: Thanks, man.

I don't have much time. Spinning on my heel, I don't realize Harlyn is behind me before I plow straight into her, gripping her arms just in time to prevent her fall.

"What are you doing back here? I thought you were getting drinks," she asks, eyeing me curiously.

"I was, then realized I needed the men's room."

She glances down the hall from where we came. "Funny because it's in the opposite direction."

I need to get her back to the ballroom, or at least the main entrance. "You're right, I just got turned around. Did you find our table?"

"Um…" Her cheeks tint red, and she lowers her gaze. "No. Sorry, I went looking for you."

"It's okay, come on. I think I saw a seating chart at the entrance." Gripping her arm lightly, we walk briskly toward the main doors. "There, over on the wall."

She heads over to the chart, and I'm a step behind, watching the door. Once I see Asher and Catarina breach the main entrance, the next few moments happen so quickly it's almost a blur.

I pull the ring from my pocket and drop to one knee. "Harlyn."

She turns, and her breath catches. Shock is what paints her face first and then a flash of anger. "Lance, what are you doing? Get up!"

Ignoring her pleas and with perfect timing, I ask the question I've wanted to for a long time. "Francis Harlyn Aldridge, will you marry me?"

"Harlyn? What's going on?" a deep voice growls from just inside the doors.

Her eyes flit to his and then to Catarina's, before her face goes white, and a hand covers her mouth.

I can't help the grin that spreads across my face at their predicament. Catarina has been filling me in on Harlyn and the teacher. It fueled the fire to make her mine. I'd originally thought it would be under different circumstances, but this is so much better than I'd expected.

Still, on one knee, I ask again, "Harlyn, will you be my wife?"

A single tear slips from her eye, and without giving him any chance to explain why he chose Catarina over her, she turns to me. "Yes, I'll marry..."

"You most certainly will not," a female voice chimes in. Gasps cast from the crowd that has now gathered around us.

It catches Harlyn's attention, and her eyes snap to the person ruining my whole plan. "Mom? Mom!" she shouts, running toward her long-lost parent and diving into her arms.

Her parents don't give two fucks about her. Why would they? The only reason they're here now is to show support of their daughter in front of everyone so it wouldn't raise any question about who took care of their darling child when they start dipping into her inheritance.

Straightening myself, I move toward my girl and her mom, but not before tossing a glance Asher's way. His stare is narrowed so hard on me, if looks could kill, I'd be murdered and then some. It warms my heart, knowing he's furious. I also flit a glance at Catarina, who only offers a small shrug, insinuating she had no idea Harlyn's parents would be here.

She and I need to talk.

"Mrs. Aldridge, so nice to see you again. I hope you had a nice flight." Laying it on thick, I focus my attention on the woman who brought my girl into this world.

Her cold stare is the only response I get before she tucks her daughter under her arm and they head down the hall. I'm left standing there alone with my grandmother's ring between my fingers and a *what the fuck were you thinking* look Harlyn tosses over her shoulder as she disappears into the nearest room.

The stares from those who stayed for the show weighs heavily against my back, but I'm not giving them the satisfaction of a breakdown. "Alright, break it up. There's nothing to see here." With a low rumble, most head toward the ballroom while others pat me on the back and give me their condolences.

Shouting turns my attention toward Asher and Catarina. "No, Catarina! I'm not doing this. Go ahead and tell your parents. Maybe you can also let them know how you blackmailed me to bring you here. Either way, I'm not staying." Yanking the door open hard, Asher practically runs out of the building and into the evening air, leaving only Catarina and me standing in the entryway—alone.

Chapter 15

Francis Harlyn Aldridge

I HOLD IT TOGETHER long enough for my mother to pull me into a private room, where as soon as I step through the door and find my dad standing by the window, the waterworks let loose. "Daddy!" I rush toward him, wrapping my arms around his waist.

"Oh, my sweet Francis, what has gotten into you?" he asks soothingly, stroking my hair.

"It seems a lot has been going on since we've been gone." I hear my mother say between my sobs. "That Freeman boy was proposing to her, and she was just about to say yes."

"Is that true, my dear?" he asks, tipping my head up so I'll meet his eyes.

Knowing I've disappointed them, all I can do is nod.

"Well, we can't have that now, can we? The Society members wouldn't approve of my daughter marrying outside of the founding families." He tucks me back close to his chest. "Sophia, see to it we have a chat with Mr. Freeman, please."

I can't see my mother, so I can only assume she's agreed to my father's request. Just as she always does.

"Come on, Harlyn, let go of your father so we can get you cleaned up and head back to the ball." She reaches for my arm. "We spent a lot of money on these tickets, so we might as well try and enjoy our time as a family."

ONCE MY DRESS HAS BEEN straightened and my makeup reapplied, the rest of the night goes as well as it can be expected. That is, given Lance's botched proposal, Asher's traitorous actions, and my mom pinching my leg every time she thinks I'll break out into tears.

Not seeing Asher anywhere is the trigger for what is most likely going to be tiny bruises all over my skin. The small nips of pain should be a welcome distraction from my thoughts of seeing him with Catarina, instead they're just another infraction to this disaster of a night.

After we've listened to the Mayor speak, and dessert is served, I'm ready to leave. "Mom, Daddy, can we go now? I'm tired and I don't feel so well."

"Not until after our father-daughter dance," he instructs.

I'd rather not do any dancing, but he's right. The Society has specific requirements of how members should act at functions, such as these. Our family needs to appear strong and uninfluenced by outside sources.

He stands up, takes my hand, and we head to the dance floor. There are a few other couples already dancing, but when we approach and without one cue from my dad, the music stops. It changes to a slow waltz; the same one my father always has them play. Selfishly, I savor the moment—the air of power the Aldridge name has over this town, it feels good. All the earlier drama dissipates into thin air with each step my father and I take around the dance floor.

"Francis, you know why we wouldn't want you marrying that low life Freeman kid, right?" His tone is harsh.

"Yes, Daddy. I know. It's frowned upon to marry anyone who's not from the founding families." There's something else I want to ask of him, and even though I'm afraid of his answer I ask anyway. "Daddy?"

"Hmmm?"

"What if a founding family member elected to work outside of the business that brought their family fortune, is that okay?"

"Well, I wouldn't say it's highly regarded, but I would expect it's acceptable." He stops mid-step, and I lift my eyes to his. "Why do you ask? Is there someone else who's shown interest in my darling daughter?"

"No, well, not really. I'm mostly curious." After a few more spins around the dance floor, the song ends and I realize I've had enough of this place. "I'm exhausted, can we go now?"

"Sure thing. I'll call the driver. You get your mother."

On the ride home, our conversation revolves around my parents gushing about their travels and the sights they've seen. I'm a bit envious, but also glad they allowed me to stay here and continue schooling. Even if they'd rather I don't graduate.

Once we're back home, I give them each a kiss on the cheek and head straight to my room, where I intend on stripping out of this dress and into the shower before settling in the soft mattress. My plan; sleep through the rest of the weekend, until Monday comes.

I'm ecstatic it's the last week of school, but I'm not looking forward to sitting through a class where both Mr. Harrington and Catarina will be.

Chapter 16

Francis Harlyn Aldridge

THE DAY I'VE DREADED is here. I somehow drag myself from the bed and get ready for school. It would be easy enough for my parents to let me stay home, but I was raised to see things through.

"Harlyn, Grace has made breakfast. Come and get it before it gets cold," Mom calls out from the base of the stairs.

It's something I'm not used to hearing since she's hardly ever here, but a nice sound, nonetheless. "Be right down."

With a final swipe of lip gloss, I leave my room and skip down the stairs two at a time. It's childish, but I'll try anything to keep from bursting into tears like I did most of yesterday. I'm not sure why seeing Asher with Catarina has this kind of effect on me. Usually, my confidence snaps back right away.

Could this be what love feels like? Am I actually in love with Winston Asher Harrington III?

It's a question I'd tossed around in my mind since the ball. I'd typically seek out Nanny Grace for answers, but now that my mother is home, she's done her best in helping me through, even though I hadn't given her the entire story. I eventually come clean about Asher being the reason I'd almost said yes to Lance; I simply hid the fact he's the same Asher they'd tried to bribe a better grade out of.

My mom's advice; don't ever stop fighting to get what I want. Her words are a double-edged sword, though. It's the exact thing she and my father are doing about my inheritance. Shrugging, I decide handling one problem at a time is all I can take for now.

The first thing I'm finding out, is what Asher was thinking when he brought that bitch to the dance.

I swipe a piece of toast off the plate Grace put together for me and rush out the door.

"Harlyn," my mom scolds.

"Sorry, gotta run. I'll see you after school."

The gears of my car strain as I push it hard down the drive and out onto the main road. I was hoping I'd get there early and chat with Asher before the first bell rings, but I don't make it. In fact, I'm late to every damn class. It's the last week of school for Christ's sake. How do they expect us to concentrate on anything, let alone learning shit that doesn't matter?

Sitting in math class, we have the same substitute teacher once again. Finding it hard to concentrate during the lecture, I glance toward the glass pane inside the classroom door and see a couple of uniformed officers pass by. The horrid chill that snakes up my spine, has me fearing, something bad has happened to Asher.

I leap from my desk passing by the stunned expressions and gasps of the students along with the surprised look on the substitute teachers face before I burst through the door. And once on the other side I see Lance directing the officers to Asher's classroom.

"Lance, what's going on?" I shout, chasing after them. When I get too close, one of the officers holds me back while another leads Asher from the room. There are no cuffs, which is a good sign, but they must be here for something.

Turning a hard stare on the man who could drop dead at this very moment and I wouldn't care, I cross my arms over my chest and ask, "Don't tell me this is some kind of revenge for me not agreeing to marry you."

Shaking his head as though my question is stupid, he turns and laughs. "Harlyn. Now that I see the real you, I'm glad you didn't. This is about Catarina. She went missing the night of the ball. The three of us were the last ones to see her. And since you're here... Officer Johnson, please bring Miss Aldridge along with us. She should be questioned, as well."

My eyes flit to Asher, and his brow creases. "Leave her out of this."

When his request goes unanswered, it's in that moment, I realize this is Lance's doing. I'm sure of it, and I won't let him get away with it. "I need to get my bag," I tell him.

"Officer Johnson, can you please get Miss Aldridge's bag from the class?"

"Yes, sir." He releases my arm and heads into the classroom.

In my moment of freedom, I rush past Lance and wrap Asher in my arms. Not missing a beat, he circles his own around me, and squeezes me tightly. The entire hall erupts with gasps and murmurs from the other students who've now gathered in the hall.

"That's enough," Lance says, pulling us apart, but not before I place a kiss on Asher's lips. My actions elicit a round of claps and whistles from the surrounding crowd, but also earns me Lance's tightened grip on my arm. "Let's go."

Chapter 17

Winston Asher Harrington III

CURRENT DAY

"Can you tell us the last time you saw Miss Mills?" Lance asks.

It's a question, if answered honestly, could put my job at risk. I consider telling them the last time I saw her was in class, but that's not the truth and he knows that. Against the recommendation of my lawyer not to say anything until he got here, I answer, "You should know, Lance, you were there." This throws him off, and he looks to the other officer. "Remember the charity ball? After Harlyn went one way and I another, I'd say that left only you, alone, with Catarina." I slide the picture back across the table. "Maybe you did this." I turn my attention to the other detective and find his glare pinned on Lance. "Have you checked the video footage at city hall?"

"Don't say another word," my family's long-time lawyer instructs as he strolls through the door. Dressed in an expensive Italian suit, his presence is like a slap in the face to both detectives. "This impromptu interrogation stops now. Any further questions you may have can be arranged through me."

He pins a hard stare on the older man. "Detective Winslow, I thought you would've known better. Mr. Harrington, get up; you're free to go."

I want to rush out of here like the entire department is on fire, but I'm not sure what Lance is capable of. With his face beginning to turn red, any quick movement may send him into a frenzy and leave me with a gunshot wound. Instead, I exit the room at a snail's pace.

With my lawyer at my side, I place a hand on his arm, stopping our descent down the police station steps. "I want to see Harlyn."

"In due time, Winston. She's back home with her parents. They've provided a solid alibi for her, and she's out of the woods; but for now, I'd recommend you keep your distance. I suspect they're going to find one of their own was the culprit here. As for his motivation, I'm sure that will be determined with time. Let's get you home and out of the public eye, until all this blows over.

Epilogue

Winston Asher Harrington III

THREE MONTHS LATER... Our wedding day

Standing at the altar, my hands shake from nerves at the anticipation of seeing her walk down the aisle. It's not the best timing as she's starting to show, but we both wanted to get married before the baby came.

Her parents and The Society had reacted better than I'd expected. They knew this child, created between two founding families—will carry on both the Aldridge and Harrington names.

Harlyn, of course, was overly excited that both hers and Quinn's baby would be born around the same time. They already have play dates planned and double baby showers.

As for Lance... it's a sad story. He was found guilty of Catarina's rape and murder, along with the help of his friend, Danny. His motives were clear; he was using her to separate Harlyn and me from being together because if I were out of the picture, he could win Harlyn back, marry her, and then collect the inheritance once she'd had an "accident."

His plan went south when he decided to kill Catarina and blame her death on me. The one thing he overlooked was that she was a society kid too. While it ultimately didn't save her life, she had learned one golden rule—always have a back-up plan. In this case, it was a recording device on a broach clipped to her skirt.

With each thrust, he was incriminating himself over and over. It sickened my stomach to hear, and I refused to let Harlyn anywhere near the recording. She's allowed the last memory of Lance as him proposing to her, but I'll not let her know what he did to that girl. It could've just as easily been her.

The dark thought dissipates instantly from my mind when I see her round the corner. She's beautiful in a white gown specially tailored to fit her curves in all the right ways and now I know there's no one I'd rather spend the rest of my life with.

Once we read our vows, and rings are placed on shaky fingers, the final words are said. "I now pronounce you husband and wife. You may kiss the bride."

It's the moment I've been waiting for, sealing our love with a kiss in front of all our family and friends.

"Please allow me to introduce to you, Mr. and Mrs. Harrington III," the preacher says.

The guests are on their feet, clapping and whistling at our union, but the celebrating stops short when a gunshot rings out.

Instantly, I grip Harlyn's arm and drag her behind some cheap wedding prop, giving her a once-over before looking out into the crowd.

Everyone is screaming and scattering in every direction.

Everyone, except Mr. Aldridge. He lies motionless on the ground, with a streak of crimson flowing aimlessly down his forehead.

Also by TL Mayhew

Belong
(Romantic Suspense - Novella)

midwest sins duet
(Dark Romance)
Taken
Found

Wicked Lady T
(Dark Romantic Suspense - Novella)
Never Lost
(Dark Romantic Suspense – Novella)

Qualify
(Contemporary Romance)

About TL Mayhew

TL Mayhew is a Contemporary and Dark Romance writer from Nebraska. Her love for reading started back in elementary school when her favorite books, The Black Stallion, Black Beauty and Misty of Chincoteague all seemed to have one theme... a horse as the leading character. It's fair to say that since then her reading tastes have changed and now, instead of a horse as the leading character it's a hot alpha.

It wasn't until she married and had two kids, that TL put any thought in to writing. And even then, it was close to a year before any words were put on paper. Amazingly those words were the direct result of a question, "Do you want to give it a try?" from an Author TL idolizes. If it weren't for that question, she may never have realized her love for writing and wouldn't have released her first work in January 2018.

Author Links

Profile: https://bit.ly/2Kxf9Xd
Page: https://www.facebook.com/tlmayhew
Group: https://bit.ly/2KyT9vm
Instagram: https://www.instagram.com/mayhewtl/
Twitter: https://twitter.com/tmayhew
Website: https://tlmayhew.com/
Bookbub: https://bit.ly/3g6otjG
TikTok: https://vm.tiktok.com/ZMeKRvgC9/